Note to parents and carers

Read it yourself is a series of classic, traditional tales, written in a simple way to give children a confident and successful start to reading.

Each book is carefully structured to include many high-frequency words that are vital for first reading. The sentences on each page are supported closely by pictures to help with reading, and to offer lively details to talk about.

The books are graded into four levels that progressively introduce wider vocabulary and longer stories as a reader's ability grows.

Ideas for use

- Begin by looking through the book and talking about the pictures. Has your child heard this story before?

- Help her with any words she does not know, either by helping her to sound them out or supplying them yourself.

- Developing readers can be concentrating so hard on the words that they sometimes don't fully grasp the meaning of what they're reading. Answering the puzzle questions on pages 30 and 31 will help with understanding.

For more information and advice, visit www.ladybird.com/readityourself

Level 2 is ideal for children who have received some reading instruction and can read short, simple sentences with help.

Special features:

Frequent repetition of main story words and phrases

Short, simple sentences

Large, clear type

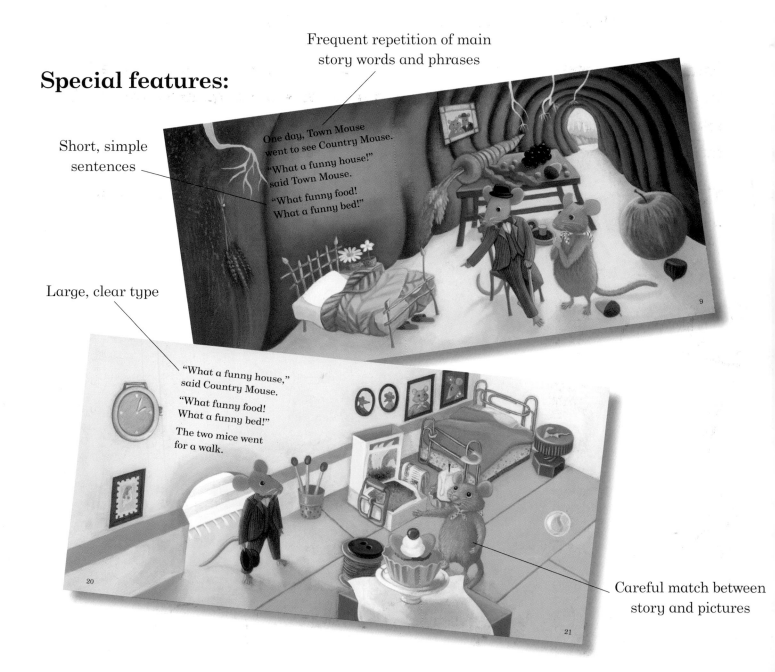

One day, Town Mouse went to see Country Mouse.

"What a funny house!" said Town Mouse.

"What funny food! What a funny bed!"

9

"What a funny house," said Country Mouse.

"What funny food! What a funny bed!"

The two mice went for a walk.

20

21

Careful match between story and pictures

Educational Consultant: Geraldine Taylor

A catalogue record for this book is available from the British Library

Published by Ladybird Books Ltd
80 Strand, London, WC2R 0RL
A Penguin Company

2 4 6 8 10 9 7 5 3 1
© LADYBIRD BOOKS LTD MMX
Ladybird, Read It Yourself and the Ladybird Logo are registered or
unregistered trade marks of Ladybird Books Limited.

ISBN: 978-1-40930-357-2

Printed in China

Town Mouse and Country Mouse

Illustrated by Alexandra Steele-Morgan

Once upon a time,
there were two mice.

Country Mouse lived
in the country.

Town Mouse lived
in the town.

One day, Town Mouse
went to see Country Mouse.

"What a funny house!"
said Town Mouse.

"What funny food!
What a funny bed!"

9

The two mice went
for a walk.

Suddenly, they heard
a noise:

Mooooooo!

"What's that?"
said Town Mouse.

"It's only a cow,"
said Country Mouse.

But Town Mouse
was very frightened.

Then they heard
another noise:

Hisssssssss!

"What's that?"
said Town Mouse.

"It's only a goose,"
said Country Mouse.

But Town Mouse
was very frightened.

Then they heard
another noise:

Whoooooooooo!

"What's that?"
said Town Mouse.

"It's the owl,"
said Country Mouse.
"Run as fast as you can!"

"I don't like it in
the country,"
said Town Mouse.

"Come with me
back to the town."

So off they went.

Town

"What a funny house,"
said Country Mouse.

"What funny food!
What a funny bed!"

The two mice went
for a walk.

Suddenly, they
heard a noise:

Parp! Parp!

"What's that?"
said Country Mouse.

"It's only a car,"
said Town Mouse.

But Country Mouse
was very frightened.

Then they heard
another noise:

Wail!

"What's that?"
said Country Mouse.

"It's only a fire engine,"
said Town Mouse.

But Country Mouse
was very frightened.

Then they heard
another noise:

Miaow!

"What's that?"
said Country Mouse.

"It's the cat!"
said Town Mouse.
"Run as fast as you can!"

And Country Mouse ran
very fast – all the way
back to the country.

Country

How much do you remember about the story of Town Mouse and Country Mouse? Answer these questions and find out!

- What makes the noise "Hiss!"?

- What makes the noise "Parp! Parp!"?

- What do the mice run away from in the country?

- What do the mice run away from in the town?

Look at the pictures and match them to
the story words.

fire engine

goose

Town Mouse

owl

Country Mouse

Read it yourself
with Ladybird

Collect all the titles in the series.